I0731580
Moonlit Redemption

Moonlit Redemption

Created by
Angel Hepburn

Table of Content

Table of Content Cont.

Chapter 1:

A Dark Home

Lilly, at the tender age of 18, bore the weight of a lifetime of abuse. Her once-bright spirit had been dimmed by the relentless darkness that enveloped her existence. Her caramel-brown hair hung in disheveled strands around her tear-streaked face, framing eyes that were once full of innocence but now held a mixture of fear and resignation.

The room she called her own was a reflection of the turmoil within her. The faded wallpaper peeled off the walls, revealing layers of forgotten dreams and broken promises. The bed, a worn-out mattress on a rusted frame, offered little comfort against the nightmares that plagued her every night. A single, dimly flickering lightbulb hung from the ceiling, casting long shadows that danced ominously around the room.

Outside her sanctuary, the sounds of her father's rage grew louder and more menacing. The harsh clinks of empty bottles crashing against the walls shattered the fragile silence, accompanied by the thunderous thuds of his boots against the worn wooden floor. Each tremor reverberated through Lilly's body, a constant reminder of the violence that awaited her beyond the confines of her room.

Her heart, battered and bruised, yearned for escape. She dreamt of a life free from the suffocating grip of her father's anger, where love and kindness were not foreign concepts. But hope had become a distant memory, a flickering flame on the verge of extinguishment. Fear had imprisoned her, chaining her to a reality that seemed destined to consume her.

But fate had a different plan in store for Lilly.

Unbeknownst to her, a powerful and mysterious force was about to intervene, shifting the course of her life forever. In the depths of her darkest night, as her father's rage reached its peak, a howl pierced through the air, cutting through the suffocating silence of her despair.

The sound was primal, filled with a raw power that stirred something deep within her. It was a call, an invitation to embrace the unknown and to venture into a world far removed from the cruelty she had known. As if guided by an invisible thread, Lilly's trembling legs carried her towards the source of that otherworldly howl.

And there, standing in the moonlit clearing just beyond the edge of the forest, was Chase—a figure that seemed both ethereal and solid, like a mythical creature brought to life. His tall frame exuded strength and confidence, his eyes a mesmerizing shade of amber that seemed to hold the secrets of the universe. His raven-black hair tumbled in wild waves, a stark contrast to the intensity in his gaze.

Chase, a werewolf who had witnessed his own share of pain and suffering, was driven by an innate need to protect the vulnerable and bring light into the darkness. It was this unwavering compassion that had drawn him to Lilly, his instincts sensing her desperate need for salvation.

As Lilly's tear-filled eyes met Chase's, a surge of warmth washed over her, like the first rays of dawn breaking through a long, cold night. In that moment, she felt a glimmer of hope, a seed of courage that began to bloom within her wounded heart. Chase extended a strong, steady hand, an offer of salvation that she hesitantly accepted.

With a single touch, their destinies intertwined, forever altering the course of their lives. The moonlit night became a witness to their shared journey, one that would lead them into a realm where love and acceptance thrived, and where darkness could be vanquished by the light of compassion.

Together, they stepped into the unknown, leaving behind the suffocating darkness that had plagued Lilly's existence. With each step, they ventured deeper into the Mystos Realm, a place where humans and supernatural creatures coexisted, and where a new chapter of Lilly's life would begin to unfold.

Chapter 2:

The Moonlit Savior

Chase's presence filled the room with an aura of strength and protection, his mere presence driving away the suffocating shadows that had haunted Lilly's existence for far too long. His muscular frame stood tall and imposing, a testament to his resilience and determination to shield those in need. He possessed an otherworldly beauty, a combination of ruggedness and grace that captivated Lilly's gaze.

His intense eyes, a mesmerizing shade of amber, seemed to hold the secrets of the universe within their depths. They bore witness to a thousand untold stories, carrying both the weight of past pain and the glimmer of future possibilities. As his gaze met Lilly's, a connection sparked between them, an unspoken understanding that transcended words.

Chase's features, chiseled and defined, revealed a life lived on the edge. His raven-black hair fell in untamed waves, brushing against his broad shoulders, a wild contrast to the controlled strength that emanated from him. His jawline was sharp, hinting at a stubborn determination that had propelled him through countless trials. With a strong, cleft chin and a faint hint of stubble, he exuded a rugged sensuality that left Lil y breathless.

In his arms, Lilly found safety and solace. His touch, gentle yet possessive, awakened dormant sensations within her, sending tingles of warmth coursing through her veins. It was as if the moonlight itself had woven a protective shield around them, shieldirg them from the outside world and creating a sacred space where vulnerability and trust could flourish.

With a single glance, Chase conveyed an unspoken promise—that he would do whatever it took to keep her safe from the darkness that had haunted her. He exuded a primal aura, a manifestation of his werewolf nature, as if he were both protector and predator, ready to defend her from any threat that dared to approach.

As Chase swept Lilly into his arms, the room faded into the background, replaced by a moonlit forest that seemed to stretch into infinity. The sounds of the night, the rustling of leaves and the distant howls, melded with the beating of their hearts, creating a symphony of passion and hope. The moon, a radiant witness to their union, cast its silver light upon their entwined bodies, illuminating their connection with a celestial glow.

For the first time in her life, Lilly felt truly seen, cherished for who she was, scars and all. In Chase's embrace, she found the strength to shed the shackles of her past, to embrace the possibility of a future filled with love and healing. In that sacred moment, she surrendered to the overwhelming tide of emotions—relief, desire, and a glimmer of happiness that had long been foreign to her wounded soul.

Their lips met in a fervent kiss, igniting a fire within them that burned brighter than the moon itself. It was a passionate embrace, filled with a longing that surpassed words. In that moment, the boundaries between human and werewolf blurred, two souls entwined in a dance as old as time itself.

As they embraced, the room transformed around them. The dilapidated walls gave way to a moonlit clearing, surrounded by ancient trees that whispered secrets in the night breeze. The air carried the scent of moss and earth, mingling with the heady fragrance of Chase's presence. It was a sanctuary, a haven where their connection could flourish without the weight of the world's judgment.

In that sacred space, Lilly's heart blossomed, her past fading into insignificance. In Chase's arms, she found the strength to embrace her true self, shedding the layers of fear and doubt that had held her captive. And in the moonlit forest, their love story unfolded, defying the darkness that had threatened to consume them both.

As the night wore on, passion and tenderness intertwined, their bodies and souls merging in a dance of ecstasy. The moon bore witness to their union, casting its silvery light upon their entangled forms. In that enchanted moment, surrounded by the mystical beauty of the Mystos Realm, Lilly and Chase embarked on a journey of healing and love, bound together by the moon's eternal embrace.

Chapter 3:

Refuge in the Pack

The hidden clearing was a sanctuary nestled deep within the heart of the ancient forest, untouched by the prying eyes of humans. Moonlight filtered through the canopy of leaves, casting an ethereal glow upon the moss-covered ground. The air was crisp, carrying the scent of damp earth and the invigorating aroma of pine. The gentle rustling of leaves and the distant hooting of an owl added a soothing symphony to the tranquil ambiance.

As Chase carried Lilly into the clearing, the pack members, their eyes gleaming with a mixture of curiosity and suspicion, gathered around, forming a protective circle. Their forms, tall and muscular, were a testament to their lycanthropic heritage. Some werewolves were adorned with intricate markings that symbolized their rank and status within the pack. Their primal energy crackled in the air, an undercurrent of strength and unity that bound them together.

At the forefront stood Gabriel, the alpha of the pack. His presence commanded attention, his regal stature and commanding aura radiating authority. With a mane of silver hair cascading down his broad shoulders, his handsome face exuded a wisdom that only centuries of experience could bestow. His eyes, a deep shade of sapphire, held a captivating mix of curiosity and protectiveness as they landed upon Lilly.

Gabriel's voice, resonant and commanding, cut through the silence. "Welcome to our pack, Lilly," he said, his tone laced with a blend of warmth and caution. "You are under our protection now."

Lilly's heart fluttered with a mix of emotions—relief, gratitude, and a hint of trepidation. She took in the werewolves' gazes, their piercing eyes searching her, assessing her worthiness to be among them. The tension in the air was palpable, a reflection of the pack's underlying uncertainty about a fragile human entering their midst.

Gabriel stepped closer, his movements deliberate and controlled. He extended a hand, his touch firm yet gentle as he brushed away a stray lock of hair from Lilly's face. His touch sent a jolt of warmth through her, an unfamiliar sensation that mingled with the lingering fear and weariness.

"Gabriel," she whispered his name, her voice tinged with vulnerability. In his eyes, she saw a glimmer of understanding, as if he recognized the pain she carried within her.

"You're safe here, Lilly," Gabriel assured her, his voice a soothing balm. "We are a family, bound by loyalty and the moon's grace. You have endured much, but know that you are no longer alone."

Lilly's heart swelled with a mix of gratitude and apprehension. She had found refuge in the pack, a place where she could heal and rebuild her shattered spirit. Yet, she couldn't help but feel the weight of their expectations, the doubt that lingered in some of their eyes.

Over time, Lilly became acquainted with the pack members. Each werewolf had their own unique personality, their quirks and strengths adding color to the tapestry of their community. Some remained cautious and reserved, keeping a watchful eye on the newcomer, while others embraced her with open arms, recognizing the strength and resilience that radiated from her.

As the days turned into weeks, Lilly immersed herself in the pack's way of life. She learned the customs and traditions, participating in their hunts and rituals, earning the respect and trust of her newfound family. She formed bonds with some of the pack members, forging friendships that helped her

navigate the complexities of her new
existence.

Gabriel, in particular, took a special interest
in Lilly's well-being. He became her guiding
light, offering guidance and protection as she
navigated the intricacies of the Mystos Realm.
With every passing day, their connection
deepened, a shared understanding and
unspoken bond forming between them.

Amidst the challenges and prejudices that
she faced as a human in a supernatural world,
Lilly found solace in Gabriel's unwavering
support. His presence, a pillar of strength and
stability, offered her a sense of belonging she
had never experienced before. In his arms, she
discovered a tenderness that healed the
wounds of her past, as well as a passion that
ignited a fire within her.

Together, they began to unravel the
mysteries of the Mystos Realm, uncovering its
hidden wonders and ancient secrets. The pack
became her family, their unity and

camaraderie a testament to the power of acceptance and the resilience of the human spirit. In their company, Lilly discovered her own inner strength, a blossoming courage that allowed her to confront the shadows of her past and embrace the light of a new beginning.

Chapter 4:

Unveiling Destinies

In the heart of the pack's territory, a grand hall stood as the gathering place for their celebrations. It was a majestic structure, adorned with intricate carvings that depicted the history and legends of their kind. The walls were adorned with tapestries, woven with threads of gold and silver, displaying scenes of valor and unity.

On this momentous occasion, the hall was filled with the flickering glow of torches and the joyful sounds of laughter and music. Pack members, their eyes alight with excitement, moved with grace and agility across the polished wooden floor. The air buzzed with anticipation as they awaited the arrival of their alpha, Gabriel, and his newfound mate, Lilly.

Gabriel, dressed in ceremonial robes that accentuated his regal presence, stood at the center of the hall. His gaze, a mix of pride and tenderness, swept across the room, taking in the faces of his pack members. His heart swelled with gratitude for their loyalty and support, but his thoughts couldn't help but be consumed by Lilly.

Lilly, radiant and breathtaking in an elegant gown, stood at Gabriel's side. Her eyes shimmered with a mixture of awe and nervousness as she surveyed the room. The vibrant colors of the decorations and the enchanting melodies of the musicians contrasted with the storm of emotions brewing within her. She couldn't deny the growing affection she felt for Gabriel, yet the memory of Chase's rescue haunted her thoughts, casting a shadow of doubt on her budding connection with the alpha.

As the celebration reached its crescendo, Gabriel took Lilly's hand in his, a gesture of unity and devotion. The room fell into a hushed silence, all eyes fixated on the couple at the heart of the gathering. With a voice that resonated with power and warmth, Gabriel addressed his pack.

"My pack, tonight is a celebration of love and unity," he began, his voice carrying the weight of his centuries-old wisdom. "Lilly has come into our lives, bringing with her a light that has illuminated our darkest corners. She is my mate, the one who completes me and brings balance to our world."

A wave of murmurs spread through the crowd, a mixture of surprise and approval. Pack members exchanged glances, their expressions a reflection of their thoughts on the human girl who had captured their alpha's heart. Some were quick to accept and embrace the union, recognizing the potential for a brighter future. Others, however, held reservations, their gazes clouded with doubt and lingering loyalty to Chase.

Among the spectators, Chase stood at the edge of the crowd, his face a mask of conflicting emotions. The joy that had once illuminated his eyes had been replaced by a simmering jealousy and a deep sense of betrayal. His heart, once filled with the hope of a future with Lilly, now burned with the pain of losing her to another. The air crackled with tension as his eyes locked with Gabriel's, a silent challenge and declaration of intent.

As the night wore on, the festivities continued, but an invisible divide settled over the pack. Whispers and sidelong glances punctuated the merriment, the underlying tension threatening to unravel the harmony that had once defined them. The delicate balance of the pack's unity hung in the balance, their loyalties tested and their destinies entwined in a complex web of love and rivalry.

In the depths of the night, beneath the moon's watchful gaze, Gabriel and Lilly found a quiet moment of respite. They stole away to a moonlit terrace, surrounded by fragrant blossoms and overlooking a serene lake. The sound of rustling leaves and the distant howls of their brethren filled the air, a reminder of the complexities that fate had woven around them.

"Lilly," Gabriel murmured, his voice carrying a blend of tenderness and uncertainty. "I understand the weight of this situation, the conflicts it stirs within you. But I promise you, my love, I will do everything in my power to protect and cherish you. Our destinies may be entangled, but the choice ultimately rests with you."

Lilly's heart swirled with a mixture of emotions as she gazed into Gabriel's eyes, searching for answers. She saw the depths of his love and the sincerity of his words, but she couldn't dismiss the haunting memory of Chase's rescue and the bond they had formed. Conflicted, she took a step back, needing time to untangle her emotions and discover her true desires.

As the moon bathed them in its silvery glow, Lilly and Gabriel stood at the precipice of their intertwined destinies, their hearts poised between loyalty, desire, and the elusive pursuit of true love. The Mystos Realm watched, holding its breath, as the fragile threads of their relationships threatened to unravel or blossom into an unbreakable bond that could transcend all obstacles.

Chapter 5:

Bonds and Betrayal

Within the heart of the pack's territory, a sprawling forest surrounded them, its ancient trees standing tall and proud, their branches intertwined like a tapestry of secrets. Sunlight filtered through the dense foliage, casting dappled shadows on the forest floor, creating a mystical ambiance that seemed to whisper tales of forgotten magic.

As Lilly navigated the complexities of her new life, she faced the skepticism and prejudice of some pack members. They questioned her place among them, citing her human nature as a weakness and a potential threat. Their mistrust manifested in subtle ways, through lingering glances and whispered conversations that echoed through the forest.

Yet, Lilly remained resolute. She refused to let their doubts define her. With each passing day, she demonstrated her resilience and unwavering spirit, proving that her worth went beyond her human origins. Her genuine kindness and compassion touched the hearts of those willing to see beyond the surface, slowly eroding the barriers of prejudice and earning her the respect she rightfully deserved.

Gabriel, torn between his duty as an alpha and his love for Lilly, found himself caught in a web of conflicting emotions. His heart ached at the division within the pack, the rift caused by Chase's jealousy and betrayal. He understood the challenges Lilly faced, and his determination to protect her only grew stronger.

Chase, consumed by his own jealousy, allowed bitterness to fester within him. The bond he had formed with Lilly, once a source of comfort and hope, now haunted his thoughts. It gnawed at him, fueling his desire for revenge against Gabriel, the one he perceived as the usurper of his love. In the depths of the forest, he plotted and schemed, driven by a wounded heart and a sense of betrayal.

As tensions rose, Lilly found solace in Gabriel's unwavering support. His love for her became a shield, protecting her from the doubts and fears that threatened to consume her. He listened to her dreams, wiped away her tears, and held her close, offering her a haven of safety amidst the storm that raged around them.

Together, Gabriel and Lilly worked tirelessly to bridge the gap between the pack members. They organized gatherings and activities, fostering a sense of unity and understanding. Through their actions, they hoped to dispel the misconceptions that fueled the prejudice against humans and pave the way for a new era of acceptance within the pack.

As time passed, small victories were won. Pack members who had once doubted Lilly began to see her for who she truly was—a beacon of strength and compassion. Bonds formed, friendships blossomed, and the pack slowly healed its wounds, their unity becoming a force to be reckoned with.

However, the impending clash between Chase and Gabriel loomed on the horizon, threatening to shatter the fragile harmony they had worked so hard to restore. The forest whispered with anticipation, the wind carrying the scent of betrayal and the weight of unspoken consequences.

In the heart of the Mystos Realm, the bonds of loyalty and the pursuit of love were tested. Lilly's presence had become a catalyst, forcing the pack to confront their prejudices and redefine their beliefs. And as the moon rose high in the night sky, casting its ethereal light upon the forest, the stage was set for a confrontation that would shape the destiny of not only Lilly, Gabriel, and Chase, but also the entire pack and the Mystos Realm itself.

Chapter 6:

Acceptance and Prejudice

The Mystos Realm, with its myriad of supernatural creatures and complex power dynamics, presented a formidable challenge for Lilly. The lingering prejudice against humans was deeply rooted in the realm's history, perpetuated by centuries of conflicts and misunderstandings. As Lilly ventured beyond the boundaries of the pack's territory, she encountered beings from various species, each harboring their own preconceived notions about humans.

In the sprawling city nestled within the Mystos Realm, towering structures melded with enchanting architecture, creating a mesmerizing blend of ancient mysticism and modern marvels. Streets bustled with creatures of all shapes and sizes, their eyes holding a mixture of curiosity and suspicion as they caught sight of Lilly. Whispers followed her, like a haunting chorus, filled with skepticism and disdain.

Lilly's heart weighed heavy with the burden of proving herself. She refused to let prejudice define her. With unwavering determination, she immersed herself in the Mystos Realm's rich tapestry of cultures, seeking knowledge and understanding. She sought out conversations with creatures of different species, listening to their stories, absorbing their wisdom, and challenging their preconceptions.

The journey of self-discovery became a kaleidoscope of emotions for Lilly. She encountered kindness and acceptance from unexpected sources, individuals who saw beyond her humanity and recognized the depth of her spirit. Their friendship and support served as a beacon of hope, fueling her resolve to bridge the gap between humans and the supernatural.

But there were moments of despair as well. Lilly faced discrimination and judgment from those who clung to their prejudices. Their disdainful gazes and cutting remarks cut deep, threatening to unravel the progress she had made. Yet, she refused to yield. With each hurtful encounter, her resilience grew, stealing her spirit and igniting a fire within her.

Lilly became a voice for change, challenging the misconceptions and stereotypes that plagued the Mystos Realm. She stood before the Council of Elders, articulating her beliefs and advocating for a world where humans and supernatural creatures could coexist in harmony. Her words resonated with some, stirring a spark of possibility, while others remained steadfast in their skepticism.

Emotions ran high within the Mystos Realm, with tensions simmering beneath the surface. The journey towards acceptance was fraught with obstacles, but Lilly's unwavering spirit and growing connections within the realm offered glimmers of hope. The seeds of change had been planted, and though the road ahead was treacherous, she remained steadfast in her belief that understanding and respect could triumph over prejudice.

As Lilly fought for acceptance, the Mystos Realm watched, teetering on the precipice of transformation. The boundaries that separated humans and supernatural creatures began to blur, giving way to a realization that unity and cooperation were vital for their mutual survival. Lilly's journey became a testament to the resilience of the human spirit, a catalyst for change in a world that had long been divided by fear and mistrust.

In the depths of the Mystos Realm, the winds of change whispered, carrying with them the promise of a future where acceptance would prevail and the barriers of prejudice would crumble. Lilly's quest to prove her worth would not only reshape the perception of humans but also challenge the very fabric of the supernatural realm itself.

Chapter 7:

Shadows of the Past

As the truth about Chase's dual nature unfolded, Lilly's heart plunged into a whirlwind of confusion and heartache. The realization that the very werewolf who had rescued her from the clutches of darkness was now her captor sent shockwaves through her soul. It was a betrayal that cut deep, fracturing the trust she had placed in him.

The environment in which she found herself reflected the darkness that now overshadowed her life. The captivity was not just physical, but also emotional, as the walls of the dimly lit chamber seemed to close in on her, suffocating her spirit. The air carried a sense of foreboding, heavy with the scent of dampness and desperation. The only source of light trickled in through a small, grated window, casting haunting shadows that danced upon the walls.

Lilly's emotions waged a fierce battle within her. She struggled with the conflicting feelings of love and betrayal that swirled within her heart. The memories of Chase's kindness and protection lingered, clashing with the stark reality of his actions. In her mind, she replayed the moments they had shared, seeking answers and trying to reconcile the person she once believed him to be with the captor before her.

It was a tumultuous journey of self-discovery, as Lilly grappled with the complexities of her emotions. The bonds she had formed with both Chase and Gabriel were tested, and she found herself torn between the two werewolves who had captured her heart. Each passing moment seemed to deepen the internal conflict, heightening her longing for freedom and a resolution to the tangled web of emotions.

The sense of captivity served as a metaphor for the entanglement of emotions that enveloped Lilly's being. The physical restraints may have held her captive, but it was the emotional ties that had the power to bind her heart and soul. The struggle between her affections for Chase, the wolf who had once been her savior, and Gabriel, the alpha who had shown her unwavering love and protection, consumed her thoughts.

In the depths of her despair, Lilly began to question the nature of love itself. Was it simply a fleeting emotion, easily overshadowed by betrayal? Or could it withstand the tests of time and circumstance? As the days turned into nights, she delved into the depths of her own soul, searching for the answers that would guide her towards a path of clarity and resolution.

Within the confines of her captivity, Lilly found solace in the memories of Gabriel's unwavering support and affection. His love had become an anchor, grounding her amidst the storm of conflicting emotions. She clung to the memories of their shared moments, the tenderness in his touch, and the depth of his understanding. It was Gabriel's love that became a beacon of hope, illuminating the darkness that threatened to consume her.

As the shadows of the past haunted her every waking moment, Lilly was faced with an agonizing choice. She had to find the strength within herself to confront her emotions head-on, to untangle the threads of love and betrayal that had become intertwined. The journey towards freedom, both physically and emotionally, awaited her, challenging her to overcome the darkness that threatened to engulf her soul.

In the depths of her captivity, Lilly's resolve began to take shape. She vowed to emerge from the shadows of the past with her spirit unbroken, determined to reclaim her autonomy and make a choice that honored her own desires and well-being. The road ahead would be treacherous, but she knew that she possessed the strength to confront her captor and the courage to forge her own path towards redemption and freedom.

Chapter 8:

Conflicting Desires

The clash of rival packs unleashed a maelstrom of chaos and violence, the air heavy with the scent of blood and the echoes of snarls and growls. Gabriel, his eyes ablaze with determination, led his loyal pack members into battle, their bodies transformed into formidable, majestic wolves. The moonlight cascaded upon their fur, lending an ethereal glow to their forms as they fought with unwavering loyalty to protect their alpha's mate.

The battleground was a vast expanse, an ancient forest that bore witness to countless battles fought throughout the ages. Towering trees stood tall, their branches reaching towards the heavens, casting long, haunting shadows upon the ground. The underbrush rustled with each passing warrior, their every step a testament to their strength and resolve. The sound of snarling and snapping jaws filled the air, mingling with the cries of pain and triumph.

Gabriel's heart pounded in his chest, fueled by a love that burned brighter than any flame. Every ounce of his being was devoted to rescuing Lilly, to safeguarding the delicate bond they had forged amidst the tumult of their intertwined destinies. His thoughts were consumed by her, his mate, whose gentle spirit had breathed life into his soul, awakening emotions he had long believed to be dormant.

As he fought with primal instinct and strategic prowess, Gabriel's mind raced with conflicting desires. On one hand, he yearned to protect and save Lilly from the clutches of Chase, to bring her back to the safety and love of their pack. Yet, deep within the recesses of his heart, a flicker of compassion and understanding burned for his rival alpha, for the wounded soul that lurked beneath Chase's façade.

In the midst of the fierce battle, the truth behind Chase's actions began to unfold, revealing a tumultuous past fraught with pain and insecurities. The scars of old wounds had driven Chase to desperate measures, to seek power and dominance at any cost. Gabriel, his heart heavy with the weight of newfound knowledge, found himself torn between a desire for vengeance and an empathetic understanding of Chase's internal torment.

Emotions ran high on the battlefield, a cauldron of conflicting desires, as the clash of fur and fangs continued. Amidst the chaos, Gabriel's loyalty to his pack and his devotion to Lilly waged an internal war, threatening to unravel his carefully constructed resolve. It was a battle not just of strength and physical prowess, but also of the heart and soul.

Meanwhile, Lilly, held captive within the tumultuous center of the conflict, felt the weight of conflicting desires and loyalties pressing upon her. The love she had once felt for Chase, the werewolf who had saved her from the darkness of her former life, collided with the profound connection she had forged with Gabriel. Her heart, a battlefield of its own, grappled with a sense of duty and the yearning for a love that felt like home.

As the battle raged on, the characters' inner struggles mirrored the chaos and turmoil that surrounded them. Gabriel's unwavering determination to save his mate and protect his pack clashed with the revelation of Chase's own internal demons. In the midst of bloodshed and strife, the boundaries between allies and enemies blurred, revealing the complexity of the supernatural world and the intricacies of the characters' desires and loyalties.

In the end, it was not just physical prowess or tactical prowess that determined the outcome of the battle, but the characters' willingness to confront their conflicting desires and find a path towards redemption and forgiveness. Through the fog of war and the clash of opposing forces, they were forced to confront their own demons and make choices that would shape their destinies.

The battlefield became a crucible of transformation, where bonds were tested and resolutions were forged. The characters, their bodies and souls battered by the intensity of the conflict, emerged changed and scarred, but with a newfound clarity and purpose. Their desires, once conflicting and fragmented, began to align with a shared understanding of the power of love, forgiveness, and the resilience of the human spirit.

Chapter 9:

The Rival Pack's Plot

Within the confines of her captivity, Lilly's spirit burned bright, refusing to be extinguished. Her resilience and unwavering determination ignited a spark of hope within the hearts of those around her, even within the rival pack itself. Whispers of dissent rippled through the ranks as some members began to question the motives and methods of their alpha.

The surroundings of Lilly's captivity were a stark contrast to the safety and warmth she had found within Gabriel's pack. Cold stone walls enclosed her, their rough texture a constant reminder of the bleakness of her situation. The air was heavy with tension, every breath tinged with the scent of fear and apprehension. In the dim light that filtered through a small, grated window, the shadows danced and twisted, mirroring the inner turmoil of those trapped within.

Emotions ran high among the captors, caught between loyalty to their alpha and a growing sympathy for Lilly. The revelation of Chase's true intentions had shattered their unquestioning trust, leaving them with a bitter taste of betrayal. Some wrestled with their own conflicting desires, torn between the loyalty they had sworn to their alpha and the empathy stirred by Lilly's courage.

In the heart of the rival pack's plot, the delicate threads that held their alliances together began to unravel. Factions emerged, each harboring their own motivations and agendas. Some sought to seize the opportunity to challenge Chase's leadership, their discontent brewing beneath the surface for far too long. Others grappled with their own moral compass, caught in a web of duty and conflicting loyalties.

As the pack's unity crumbled, tensions escalated to dangerous heights. Whispers turned into murmurs, murmurs into disagreements, and disagreements into outright confrontations. The once-unified pack became a battleground of ideologies and personal vendettas, threatening to tear them apart from within.

For Lilly, the situation was both a test of her inner strength and an opportunity for unexpected alliances. As she navigated the treacherous landscape of her captivity, she found solace in the unlikely friendships she forged with individuals who had once been her captors. The shared desire for freedom and the disillusionment with their alpha's actions united them, binding them in a common cause.

Amidst the chaos, the characters were forced to confront their own perceptions of themselves and each other. The lines between friend and foe blurred, as hidden depths of compassion and understanding were revealed. Preconceived notions and prejudices were challenged, giving rise to a glimmer of empathy and the possibility of redemption.

In the midst of this intricate web of deceit and shifting alliances, the characters were faced with difficult choices. Some struggled to reconcile their loyalty to their pack with their growing empathy for Lilly, while others grappled with their own desires for power and recognition. The fragile balance between their own sense of identity and the expectations imposed upon them by their respective roles began to tremble.

As the rival pack's plot unraveled, it became evident that the true battle was not just against external forces, but the inner demons that haunted the characters. In this crucible of conflicting emotions and shattered loyalties, they were forced to confront their own flaws, question their beliefs, and seek a path towards reconciliation and redemption.

Chapter 10:

Captured by Darkness

Captured by the darkness of her own conflicted emotions, Lilly stood at the precipice of an impossible choice. Her heart, torn between Chase and Gabriel, ached with a longing for love, acceptance, and a sense of belonging that had eluded her for so long. The weight of the world seemed to rest upon her fragile shoulders as the fate of the Mystos Realm hung in the balance.

Surrounded by the remnants of the battle, the battlefield itself became a reflection of Lilly's internal turmoil. The air crackled with residual energy, the scent of blood and sweat mingling with the earthy aroma of the forest. Fallen leaves, once vibrant and full of life, now lay scattered like shattered dreams, a stark reminder of the consequences of their choices.

In the aftermath of the conflict, the characters stood battered and weary, their faces etched with the marks of their struggles. Each step they took on the blood-soaked ground was a testament to their resilience, their determination to overcome the darkness that threatened to consume them all.

Emotions ran rampant, like wildfire in their hearts. Lilly's mind became a battlefield of its own, as memories of her past collided with her hopes for the future. Fear intermingled with longing, doubt tangled with desire, and love wrestled with betrayal. The echoes of her father's abuse still haunted her, leaving scars that ran deeper than any physical wounds.

For Chase, his jealousy and anger simmered beneath the surface, transforming into a maelstrom of conflicting emotions. He grappled with the realization that his actions had caused pain and suffering, not only for Lilly but also for those he had once considered his pack. Regret gnawed at his soul as he yearned for redemption, seeking a way to make amends for his past transgressions.

Gabriel, on the other hand, was consumed by a sense of responsibility and a burning desire to protect what was rightfully his. The love he felt for Lilly surged through his veins, intertwining with the weight of his duty as an alpha. He understood the consequences of their choices and the impact it would have on their world. His heart bled for Lilly, knowing that her decision would determine not only their fate but also the fragile balance of power in the Mystos Realm.

Surrounded by the remnants of the battle, the characters found themselves in a moment of reflection and introspection. The scars they bore, both seen and unseen, became a testament to the sacrifices they had made and the lengths they were willing to go for the ones they loved. In this crucible of darkness, they were forced to confront their deepest

fears and confront the truth of who they truly
were.

As Lilly stood at the crossroads of her destiny,
she yearned for guidance and clarity. Her soul
craved the light that would guide her towards
a future filled with love, compassion, and a
sense of purpose. The weight of her decision
pressed upon her like an insurmountable
burden, knowing that whatever path she
chose would forever shape the lives of those
around her.

In this pivotal moment, the Mystos Realm
held its breath, its very existence hanging in
the balance. It was a time of reckoning, where
the shadows of the past intertwined with the
hope of a brighter future. The characters, their
hearts laid bare, awaited the decision that
would ultimately define their intertwined
destinies.

Chapter 11:

Trials and Tribulations

In the dark confines of her captivity, Lilly's spirit refused to be extinguished. Bound and confined, she faced a series of trials designed to break her resolve, to strip away her hope and force her surrender. The walls of her prison closed in, suffocating her as each day tested her physical and emotional endurance

Surrounded by shadows and silence, Lilly's only solace was the memories of her time with Gabriel, the touch of his hand, and the warmth of his love. It was these memories that fueled her determination, that reminded her of the strength she carried within. Their love had become an anchor, grounding her in the face of adversity.

The trials she faced were a relentless assault on her spirit. They challenged her physical limits, pushing her body to the brink of exhaustion. Through grueling physical tasks, she endured, refusing to let the pain and fatigue break her. She summoned an inner strength she never knew she possessed, drawing upon the love and protection she had experienced from Gabriel. It was in these moments of struggle that she discovered the depths of her resilience.

But the trials were not only physical; they were emotional as well. Lilly was subjected to psychological torment, her captors seeking to exploit her fears and insecurities. They taunted her with memories of her past, dredging up the pain and trauma she had fought so hard to overcome. Yet, amidst the torment, she clung to the love that had blossomed between her and Gabriel, using it as a shield against the darkness that threatened to consume her.

In the midst of her trials, unexpected allies emerged from the shadows. Kindred souls who had also suffered at the hands of their captors rallied around Lilly, forming a bond forged in shared pain and a shared desire for freedom. Together, they supported and encouraged one another, offering a glimmer of hope in the midst of their despair. Through their unity, they found strength, realizing that they were not alone in their struggles.

As the trials intensified, Lilly's determination grew fiercer. She refused to be broken, to let the trials define her. With each passing day, she discovered new facets of her character, tapping into depths of courage and resilience she never thought possible. The love she had experienced with Gabriel had ignited a fire within her, and it burned brighter with each trial she faced.

In the face of danger and uncertainty Lilly's spirit shone like a beacon of hope. She became a symbol of resilience and determination, inspiring those around her to never give up, to keep fighting against all odds. Her unwavering spirit and the support of her allies became a source of strength that sustained them through the darkest moments.

Through the trials and tribulations, Lilly's journey became a testament to the indomitable power of love and the strength of the human spirit. She refused to be defined by her captivity; instead, she forged her own path, determined to reclaim her freedom and rewrite her destiny. The trials tested her, shaped her, and ultimately empowered her to rise above the darkness that sought to consume her.

And as Lilly emerged from the trials, battered but unbroken, she carried within her a renewed sense of purpose and a deeper understanding of her own strength. With each step forward, she drew closer to the ultimate confrontation that would determine the fate of the Mystos Realm and the fulfillment of her intertwined destinies.

Chapter 12:

Unmasking the True Alpha

Amidst the tumultuous chaos that surrounded them, the truth behind Chase's actions finally came to light, exposing the intricate web of pain and insecurities that had driven him down a treacherous path. As the layers of his deception were peeled away, Lilly found herself standing face-to-face with a complex and tormented soul.

The revelation of Chase's true motivations shattered Lilly's perception of him, leaving her reeling with a mix of shock, confusion, and a deep sense of betrayal. The man she had once admired, the werewolf who had rescued her from darkness, had been consumed by his own inner demons. The pain etched across his face, the haunted look in his eyes, it all painted a picture of a soul tormented by past wounds.

In that moment, Lilly's emotions swirled within her like a tempest. Anger, disappointment, and hurt collided, threatening to overwhelm her. How could she have been so blind to the darkness that lurked beneath Chase's heroic facade? The trust she had placed in him crumbled, leaving behind a void filled with a mix of bitterness and heartache.

Yet, amidst the storm of emotions, a flicker of compassion burned within Lilly's heart. She began to understand that Chase's actions were born out of his own pain and insecurities, a desperate attempt to fill the void within his soul. In that realization, a seed of empathy took root, and she found herself torn between her desire for justice and the growing understanding that redemption was possible, even for someone lost in the depths of darkness.

As Lilly delved deeper into Chase's past, she discovered the wounds that had shaped him, the scars that had driven him to seek power and dominance. The revelations unveiled a broken individual haunted by a sense of inadequacy, driven to prove his worth at any cost. It became clear that his actions were not solely driven by malice but were born out of a desperate need for validation and acceptance.

With each revelation, Lilly's perception of love and forgiveness underwent a profound transformation. She realized that true redemption required confronting inner demons, acknowledging the pain that resided within, and embarking on a journey of healing. It was a lesson that extended beyond Chase's story, penetrating deep into her own soul. She recognized the need to face her own fears and confront the wounds that had shaped her own journey.

In the midst of this emotional turmoil, Lilly discovered that forgiveness did not mean forgetting or condoning the hurtful actions of others. It meant finding the strength to release the grip of anger and resentment, to let go of the chains that bound her to the pain of the past. It was a difficult and complex process, but she understood that it was a necessary step toward her own healing and growth.

As Lilly grappled with conflicting emotions and confronted the true depths of Chase's darkness, she also found solace in the unwavering support of Gabriel and the pack. They stood by her side, offering strength and guidance, reminding her of the love and light that existed amidst the shadows. Through their unwavering loyalty, she discovered the power of a chosen family, of finding solace and strength in the bonds forged through shared experiences.

In the midst of this transformative journey, Lilly's own resilience and capacity for compassion expanded. She became a beacon of hope, an embodiment of the belief that even the darkest souls could find redemption and forgiveness. Through her own struggles and the challenges she faced, she became a testament to the transformative power of love and the human spirit.

Chapter 13:

Torn Between Two Alphas

Lilly stood at the precipice of a heart-wrenching decision, torn between the two alphas who had captured her heart in different ways. On one side stood Gabriel, his unwavering love and devotion offering her stability, safety, and a future filled with passion and tenderness. On the other side stood Chase, the werewolf who had once been her savior, now standing before her vulnerable and remorseful, desperately seeking a chance at redemption.

Gabriel's presence enveloped her like a warm embrace, his eyes filled with unwavering love and understanding. With him, she had discovered a love that transcended boundaries, a love that brought solace and ignited a flame within her soul. He had been her rock, offering unwavering support and protection, a sanctuary in the storm that had threatened to consume her. His love was a steady force, anchoring her in a world filled with uncertainties.

But as Lilly gazed into Chase's eyes, she saw a reflection of her own pain and longing for redemption. He stood before her stripped of the bravado that had once masked his insecurities, baring his soul in search of forgiveness. The raw vulnerability in his eyes tugged at her heart, stirring up a torrent of conflicting emotions. She couldn't deny the bond they had shared, the connection that had once saved her from the darkness. A part of her still longed to believe that he could find his way back to the light.

In the midst of this emotional whirlwind, Lilly found herself delving deep into her heart, seeking answers to the questions that plagued her. What did she truly desire? Was it the stability and love that Gabriel offered, or was it the possibility of redemption and a second chance with Chase?

The surroundings mirrored her inner turmoil. The air crackled with tension, the atmosphere charged with the weight of her decision. The moon cast a pale glow upon the landscape, its light casting long shadows that danced like whispers of uncertainty. Nature itself seemed to hold its breath, as if aware of the pivotal moment that would shape not only Lilly's destiny but the fate of the Mystos Realm.

Emotions raged within her, each vying for dominance. Love, fear, forgiveness, and self-discovery intertwined in a tumultuous dance. She feared making the wrong choice, afraid of causing further pain or repeating past mistakes. Doubt gnawed at her, threatening to drown out the voice of her own desires.

In the quiet moments of introspection, Lilly confronted the depths of her own heart. She recognized that her journey was not just about choosing between two alphas, but about discovering her own path to healing and self-acceptance. She yearned to break free from the confines of expectations and societal norms, to forge her own destiny.

It was in the depths of her soul-searching that Lilly unearthed the truth that had been simmering within her all along. She realized that her heart longed for the love she had found with Gabriel, a love built on trust, stability, and the promise of a future filled with warmth and understanding. It was with him that she felt the deepest sense of belonging, a love that nurtured and encouraged her growth.

As the realization settled within her, a mix of relief and sadness washed over Lilly. She knew that choosing Gabriel meant leaving behind the possibility of redeeming Chase, of rekindling the connection they once shared. It was a bittersweet acceptance, a letting go of what could have been.

With her decision made, Lilly took a step forward, her heart filled with both conviction and compassion. She approached Chase, her voice steady as she spoke of forgiveness, of the possibility of finding redemption on his own journey. She offered him a lifeline, a glimmer of hope to guide him toward a path of healing and self-discovery, even if it meant doing so apart from her.

And as the moon hung high in the sky, casting its pale glow upon the tumultuous scene, Lilly took Gabriel's hand, intertwining their fingers. Together, they faced the uncertain future with hearts full of love and determination, ready to forge a destiny rooted in the strength of their bond and the power of their love.

Chapter 14:

Battle for Freedom

The air crackled with electric energy as the rival packs converged upon the battlefield. Lilly stood shoulder to shoulder with Gabriel, their hands tightly clasped, as they faced the daunting task ahead. The surroundings were transformed into a chaotic battleground, with trees splintering under the force of supernatural powers and the earth trembling beneath their feet. Dark clouds gathered overhead, casting a shadow over the battleground, mirroring the intensity of the conflict that was about to unfold.

Emotions ran high, a volatile mix of determination, fear, and adrenaline coursing through their veins. Lilly's heart pounded in her chest, each beat echoing the resolute resolve that had settled within her. She could feel the weight of the battle, the stakes so high that they threatened to suffocate her. But she refused to let fear consume her. She drew strength from the love she shared with Gabriel, from the unbreakable bond that had sustained them throughout their journey.

As the battle commenced, supernatural powers collided, filling the air with dazzling displays of light and shadow. Werewolves lunged and clashed, their fangs bared, while other creatures unleashed elemental forces that tore through the battlefield. The clash of steel and the crackle of energy echoed through the night, as each combatant fought with unyielding determination.

In the midst of the chaos, loyalties were tested and friendships were forged. Allies who had once stood on opposite sides now fought side by side, their shared goal of freedom binding them together. They formed an intricate tapestry of unity, each individual bringing their unique strengths to the forefront, fighting for a chance at a better future.

Sacrifices were made in the name of love and the pursuit of liberty. Characters pushed themselves to the limits, willingly putting their lives on the line to protect one another and preserve the fragile balance of the Mystos Realm. The battlefield became a testament to their resilience, marked by the fallen and the wounded, a stark reminder of the price they were willing to pay for the hope of a brighter tomorrow.

Amidst the chaos, Lilly's heart swelled with a mix of determination and compassion. She fought with unwavering resolve, her every move fueled by the love she held for her allies and the burning desire to protect the life she had built alongside Gabriel. Each strike, each defensive maneuver, carried with it a fierce determination to overcome the forces that sought to oppress them.

As the battle reached its crescendo, the tides of fate turned in their favor. The rival pack's resistance wavered, their forces dwindling under the relentless assault of Lilly, Gabriel, and their allies. Victory seemed within reach, a shimmering beacon of hope in the midst of darkness.

But the battle was not without its losses. Characters who had become dear to Lilly and Gabriel fell in the line of duty, their sacrifices etched forever in their hearts. The weight of their absence served as a constant reminder of the fragility of life and the price they had paid for their freedom.

In the final moments of the battle, as the rival pack's forces crumbled, Lilly and Gabriel stood together, their bodies battered and weary, but their spirits unyielding. The sense of accomplishment mingled with a bittersweet realization that their journey was far from over. The battle had been won, but the aftermath would require healing, rebuilding, and forging a new path forward.

With their heads held high and their hearts brimming with hope, Lilly and Gabriel surveyed the aftermath of the battle. The once-ominous surroundings now bore the scars of the conflict, a testament to the strength and resilience of those who had fought for their freedom. They took solace in the knowledge that their sacrifices had not been in vain, that they had paved the way for a future where love, unity, and understanding could prevail.

As they embraced amidst the wreckage, a mix of relief and determination washed over them. They knew that the battle for freedom was ongoing, that new challenges would arise, but they were prepared to face whatever came their way. Hand in hand, they embarked on the next chapter of their journey, fortified by the bonds they had forged and the unbreakable love that fueled their spirits.

Chapter 15:

Confronting the Demons Within

The aftermath of the battle brought a somber stillness to the surroundings, as the characters surveyed the wreckage that lay in their wake. The once-vibrant landscape was marred by the scars of the conflict, serving as a poignant reminder of the toll the war had taken on their lives. The air was heavy with a mix of exhaustion, sorrow, and a flicker of hope for what lay ahead.

Lilly, Gabriel, and Chase, each carrying their own burdens, embarked on a profound journey of self-discovery. They sought to confront the demons within themselves, to understand the wounds that had driven their choices and actions. The path they walked was one of introspection and reflection, requiring them to delve into the depths of their pasts and face the uncomfortable truths that lay hidden.

Emotions ran deep as they navigated the intricate landscape of forgiveness, redemption, and personal growth. Lilly, haunted by the trauma of her captivity and torn between her love for Gabriel and the complicated history she shared with Chase, grappled with conflicting emotions. Her heart yearned for resolution, for healing, but she knew that it would require confronting the darkest corners of her own psyche.

Gabriel, the regal and steadfast alpha, found himself torn between the desire to protect Lilly and the need to come to terms with his own vulnerabilities. The scars of past wounds and centuries of solitude had shaped his perception of himself, and he yearned for a future where he could fully embrace love and vulnerability without fear. His journey of self-discovery paralleled Lilly's, as they both sought to find a way to reconcile their pasts and forge a future together.

Chase, once a symbol of strength and protection, confronted the depths of his own pain and insecurities. The revelation of his true motivations had shattered the trust of those around him, and he faced a crucial turning point in his journey. Fueled by remorse and a burning desire for redemption, he sought to confront his demons head-on, to understand the root of his actions, and to find a path toward healing and reconciliation.

The characters faced their personal demons with a mixture of trepidation and determination. They sought guidance from wise mentors within their pack, who provided a safe space for introspection and offered invaluable insights. Together, they explored the complexities of their own histories, unraveling the layers of their past traumas, and understanding how these experiences had shaped their present selves.

Through moments of vulnerability and raw honesty, they gradually peeled back the layers of their pain, exposing their deepest fears and regrets. Emotions spilled over, ranging from anger and guilt to forgiveness and acceptance. Each step on their journey brought them closer to understanding the complexities of their own identities and the motivations that had driven their actions.

As the characters confronted their demons, their relationships underwent profound transformations. Trust, once shattered, began to mend, as they embarked on a path of healing and understanding. Their interactions were filled with raw, authentic conversations, where they acknowledged the mistakes of the past and embraced the opportunity for growth and redemption.

The surroundings mirrored their inner turmoil, alternating between serene moments of reflection amidst the remnants of nature's beauty and turbulent storms that mirrored the emotional turbulence they experienced. The natural world became a metaphor for their journey, symbolizing the cycle of destruction and rebirth, and the inherent resilience of the human spirit.

As they confronted their demons and made peace with their pasts, the characters gradually found solace within themselves and within their relationships. They recognized that healing was not a linear process, but a series of steps forward and occasional setbacks. Through vulnerability, understanding, and unwavering support, they forged a path towards personal growth and redemption.

Chapter 16:

Redemption and Forgiveness

In the wake of their individual journeys of self-discovery and the collective confrontation of their demons, the characters found themselves standing at the precipice of redemption and forgiveness. The weight of their past actions and the consequences of their choices hung heavy in the air, yet a glimmer of hope illuminated their path forward.

Surrounded by the natural beauty of the Mystos Realm, they gathered in a serene clearing, the tranquil setting reflecting the calmness that had settled within their hearts. The air was filled with a sense of anticipation, a collective understanding that they stood on the threshold of transformation and healing.

Emotions ran deep as they engaged in honest and vulnerable conversations, laying bare their regrets, acknowledging the pain they had caused, and expressing genuine remorse. Each character took turns sharing their reflections, their voices laden with a mixture of guilt, sadness, and an earnest desire for redemption.

Lilly, guided by her newfound strength and understanding, opened her heart to forgiveness. She recognized that holding onto anger and resentment would only perpetuate the cycle of pain. With tearful eyes and a tremble in her voice, she extended forgiveness to Chase for the harm he had caused, acknowledging that he too was a product of his own past wounds.

Chase, humbled and transformed by the depth of his own self-reflection, accepted responsibility for his actions. Overwhelmed with remorse, he listened intently to Lilly's words, his own eyes welling with tears. In that moment, he glimpsed the possibility of redemption and a chance to rebuild the trust he had shattered.

Gabriel, who had weathered the storm with unwavering support and steadfast love, recognized the power of forgiveness as an essential catalyst for personal growth. He, too, sought forgiveness from those he had unintentionally hurt with his guardedness and stoicism. With a mixture of humility and gratitude, he embraced the opportunity to evolve into a more vulnerable and open-hearted leader.

As forgiveness permeated the atmosphere, a profound sense of relief and catharsis washed over the characters. The weight that had burdened their souls began to lift, making way for a renewed sense of hope and possibility. They realized that redemption was not about erasing the past, but about using it as a foundation for growth and positive change.

Within the embrace of forgiveness, bonds that had once been fractured began to mend. The characters approached each other with newfound understanding, compassion, and an unwavering commitment to support one another's journeys. Walls of distrust crumbled, and bridges of connection were built, forging a unity that would prove vital in the trials that lay ahead.

The surroundings mirrored this transformative moment, as if nature itself celebrated the healing that took place. The sunlight broke through the canopy, casting a warm glow on the clearing, symbolizing the dawn of a new chapter. The gentle breeze whispered words of encouragement, carrying with it the promise of a future where love, trust, and unity flourished.

With forgiveness as their guiding light, the characters embarked on a collective path of redemption. They understood that the road would not be without challenges, but armed with the lessons of their past, they were prepared to face whatever obstacles lay ahead. They knew that the healing process required continued effort, vulnerability, and a commitment to learning from their mistakes.

In this chapter, redemption and forgiveness became catalysts for personal growth and the mending of relationships. It served as a reminder that no one was defined solely by their past, but rather by their capacity to acknowledge mistakes, seek forgiveness, and strive to become better versions of themselves.

As they embraced redemption and forgiveness, the characters discovered the power of second chances and the transformative nature of compassion. They embraced a future where love, trust, and unity thrived, determined to create a world where the shadows of their pasts would no longer define them.

Chapter 17:

Choosing the Path of Love

Lilly stood at the crossroads of her destiny, her heart heavy with the weight of her decision. The air crackled with anticipation as she surveyed the world around her, the Mystos Realm itself seemingly holding its breath. The vibrant hues of the forest painted a tapestry of nature's beauty, serving as a backdrop to this pivotal moment in her life.

Emotions swirled within Lilly's being, a tumultuous mix of love, fear, and a yearning for a future that embraced both her humanity and the supernatural world she had come to understand. Her journey had brought her to this critical juncture, where she had to choose between two distinct paths, each offering its own promises and challenges.

On one side stood Chase, his gaze filled with remorse and a desperate plea for forgiveness. Memories of their past intertwined with her present reality, blurring the lines between friendship, loyalty, and the lingering traces of an affection that once burned brightly. Yet, the wounds inflicted upon her heart by his actions were still fresh, and the shadows of mistrust lingered in her mind.

On the other side stood Gabriel, his presence radiating strength, compassion, and an unwavering love that had weathered the storms of doubt and tribulation. His eyes, filled with tenderness and determination, mirrored the promises he had made to protect her, to nurture a relationship built on trust and equality. Their connection had deepened through shared experiences, moments of vulnerability, and a profound understanding of each other's flaws and strengths.

As she contemplated her decision, the weight of responsibility bore down upon her.

The Mystos Realm yearned for a leader, someone who could bridge the gap between humans and supernatural creatures, ushering in an era of coexistence and harmony. Lilly recognized the profound impact her choice would have on the lives of those around her and the fragile balance between these two worlds.

In her heart, she knew that love was not merely an emotion but a transformative force capable of shaping destinies and bringing about profound change. It was this realization that guided her decision, leading her to choose the path of love embodied by Gabriel. She saw in him a partner, an ally, and a champion of understanding, who would stand by her side as they faced the challenges ahead.

As the words left her lips, a mix of relief and sorrow washed over Lilly. She understood that in choosing Gabriel, she would inevitably leave behind a part of her past, a bond that had once held meaning and promise. Yet, she also knew that this decision was not only for her own happiness but for the greater good of the Mystos Realm.

Surrounding them, the natural world seemed to respond to the energy of Lilly's choice. Sunlight filtered through the canopy, casting warm rays that danced upon her skin, illuminating the path before her. The gentle rustle of leaves whispered words of affirmation, as if nature itself acknowledged and embraced her decision.

Emotions ran high among the characters present, each holding their own stake in the outcome. Chase, though pained by the rejection, recognized the depth of his own transgressions and the need for personal growth. He respected Lilly's decision, even if it meant relinquishing the dreams he had once held.

Gabriel, his eyes shining with a mixture of gratitude and love, extended his hand towards Lilly. It was a silent invitation to step forward into a shared future, built on trust, understanding, and a commitment to upholding the values they held dear. The bonds between them grew stronger as they embarked on a journey that would shape not only their own lives but the destiny of the Mystos Realm.

With her choice made, Lilly embraced the path of love, fully aware of the challenges and sacrifices that lay ahead. Together with Gabriel, she would strive to bring about reconciliation, unity, and acceptance between humans and supernatural creatures, breaking the cycle of fear and prejudice that had plagued their world for far too long.

As they took their first steps forward, a sense of hope radiated from their joined hands, their hearts beating in unison. The echoes of their decision reverberated throughout the Mystos Realm, signaling the beginning of a new era—a testament to the transformative power of love and the indomitable spirit of those who dared to follow its path.

Chapter 18:

Healing and Rebuilding

The aftermath of the climactic battle left the Mystos Realm scarred, both physically and emotionally. The once vibrant landscapes were marred by the remnants of destruction, serving as a constant reminder of the trials endured. Amidst the wreckage, the characters banded together, their shared purpose driving them to mend what had been broken and rebuild a world that had been fractured by fear and animosity.

Lilly, Gabriel, and their allies became beacons of hope, leading the charge in healing the wounds inflicted upon the Mystos Realm. Their determination to foster unity and understanding resonated with others, inspiring a collective effort towards reconciliation. They organized work groups, comprising both humans and supernatural creatures, to restore the damaged territories, mending the physical scars left behind by the battles fought.

Emotions ran deep during this process of healing and rebuilding. The characters faced their own inner demons and grappled with the aftermath of the conflicts they had endured. There were moments of introspection, where each individual reflected on their choices, their contributions to the strife, and the personal growth they had achieved. Guilt, remorse, and a desire for redemption mingled with feelings of hope, resilience, and the belief in a brighter future.

The Mystos Realm itself seemed to respond to their efforts, gradually shedding its desolate façade. Nature, resilient and ever-adaptive, began to reclaim its beauty, as vibrant flora sprouted from the once barren landscapes. Animals returned, their presence symbolizing the restoration of balance and the resurgence of life. Sunsets painted the sky with hues of warmth and serenity, offering solace to those who had endured the trials of conflict.

But healing extended beyond the physical realm. Emotional wounds required delicate care and understanding. The characters engaged in heartfelt conversations, openly sharing their experiences and vulnerabilities. They embraced the power of empathy and active listening, fostering an environment of support and acceptance. Through these dialogues, prejudices were dismantled, biases were challenged, and the foundations of trust were rebuilt.

The healing process was not without its challenges. Lingering doubts and lingering resentments occasionally threatened to disrupt the fragile harmony they had achieved. Yet, the characters persevered, recogn zing that healing was a continuous journey. They remained committed to the shared vision of a Mystos Realm free from discrimination and fear, where the diversity of its inhabitants was celebrated as a source of strength.

As time passed, their efforts bore fruit. The Mystos Realm began to flourish once more, transformed by the collective determination to create a world that honored both humans and supernatural creatures. New alliances were forged, as individuals from different backgrounds and species united in pursuit of a common goal.

With each passing day, acts of kindness and understanding became the norm, replacing animosity with empathy, suspicion with trust. Communities emerged where humans and supernatural creatures coexisted harmoniously, celebrating the unique qualities that made each being special. The scars of the past served as reminders of the resilience and triumph that could arise from adversity.

In this renewed Mystos Realm, Lilly and Gabriel's love served as a guiding light, illuminating the path towards a future where love, acceptance, and unity prevailed. Their bond not only symbolized the power of personal connection but also stood as a testament to the potential for growth and change within each individual.

The healing and rebuilding process was not without setbacks, but the characters remained steadfast in their resolve. They understood that healing was not a destination but an ongoing journey, requiring continuous effort, understanding, and a commitment to nurturing the bonds that held their world together.

As the Mystos Realm embraced its transformed identity, the characters reveled in the beauty of their collective achievement. They had overcome the shadows of the past, sowed the seeds of compassion, and together, they had built a future where hope, love, and acceptance reigned supreme.

Chapter 19:

Embracing a New Destiny

Lilly and Gabriel, united by their unwavering love and a shared vision of harmony, embarked on a new chapter in their lives—one that would bridge the gap between the Mystos Realm and the human world. As ambassadors of change, they embraced their destiny with passion and determination, eager to break down the barriers that had long divided these two realms.

Surrounded by the breathtaking beauty of the Mystos Realm, Lilly and Gabriel began their mission. They sought to foster understanding and acceptance between supernatural creatures and humans, recognizing that knowledge and empathy were the key to dismantling prejudice and fear.

Their journey took them to bustling cities, quiet rural communities, and everywhere in between. With each interaction, they shared stories of the Mystos Realm's inhabitants, painting a vivid picture of the diverse supernatural creatures that coexisted alongside humans. They showcased the profound abilities and wisdom possessed by these beings, debunking misconceptions and challenging preconceived notions.

As they engaged with humans, emotions ran high. Lilly and Gabriel encountered a spectrum of reactions—curiosity, skepticism, and even fear. Some embraced their message with open hearts, eager to expand their understanding of the supernatural. Others clung to their deeply ingrained prejudices, hesitant to let go of long-held beliefs. Yet, the couple remained steadfast, approaching each encounter with patience, empathy, and an unwavering belief in the power of education and compassion.

Surroundings played a crucial role in their efforts. They sought out spaces where diverse groups of individuals could come together, fostering dialogue and promoting mutual respect. In parks, community centers, and even virtual platforms, they organized gatherings where humans and supernatural creatures shared their experiences, fears, and dreams. These environments, filled with the sounds of shared laughter and heartfelt conversations, became catalysts for change, eroding the walls that had long separated the two worlds.

Amidst the challenges, there were moments of profound connection. Lilly and Gabriel witnessed the transformative power of personal encounters, where understanding blossomed and barriers crumbled. Humans and supernatural creatures discovered common ground, realizing that their differences were not to be feared but celebrated. Through shared stories, shared struggles, and shared triumphs, bridges were built, and bonds were formed.

Emotions ran deep as Lilly and Gabriel continued to navigate this delicate path. They carried the weight of their responsibility, knowing that the success of their mission would impact the lives of countless individuals. There were moments of doubt, when the enormity of the task at hand threatened to overwhelm them. But in these moments, they drew strength from each other, reaffirming their commitment to their shared purpose.

Together, Lilly and Gabriel exemplified the love and acceptance they sought to cultivate. Their relationship became a beacon of hope, proving that love transcended boundaries and that unity was possible even in the face of adversity. Their unwavering bond inspired others to examine their own biases, to question the limitations they had placed on themselves and the world around them.

In the Mystos Realm and beyond, a ripple effect of change began to take hold. The walls of fear and mistrust crumbled, replaced by bridges of understanding and compassion. The human world started to embrace the beauty and magic of the supernatural, while the Mystos Realm learned to appreciate the complexities and strengths of human existence.

As time passed, the realms grew closer, their boundaries blurring as understanding deepened. Humans and supernatural creatures coexisted with newfound respect and appreciation, collaborating on projects that celebrated the fusion of their unique talents and perspectives. Schools and educational institutions incorporated courses on supernatural studies, promoting inclusivity and fostering a sense of wonder and interconnectedness.

In the midst of this transformation, Lilly and Gabriel continued to nurture their own love

and commitment. They stood side by s de,
their shared experiences and triumphs
strengthening their bond. Together, they
embraced their new destiny, forever grateful
for the opportunity to shape a world where
acceptance, empathy, and love reigned
supreme.

Chapter 20:

Epilogue: Moonlit Forever

In the serene tranquility of the Mystos Realm, time flowed gracefully, weaving stories of love and transformation. Lilly and Gabriel stood as beacons of hope and symbols of the enduring power of their shared love. Their journey, filled with trials and triumphs, had left an indelible mark on the Mystos Realm and its inhabitants.

Surrounded by the breathtaking beauty of the mystical realm, Lilly and Gabriel found their home in a secluded cottage nestled amidst ancient trees and fragrant flowers. The walls of their sanctuary were adorned with cherished memories, capturing moments of joy, growth, and unity. The enchanting moonlight spilled through the windows, casting a soft glow on their shared history.

Emotions washed over them in waves, as they reflected on their remarkable journey. They had witnessed the transformation of the Mystos Realm, from a place marred by fear and division to a harmonious sanctuary where humans and supernatural creatures thrived side by side. The once fractured bonds had been mended, and a tapestry of unity had been woven, held together by the enduring power of acceptance and respect.

Lilly's heart brimmed with contentment and fulfillment. The trials she had faced, the choices she had made, had led her to this moment. She had come to understand that her destiny was not simply about finding love or bridging two worlds—it was about leaving a lasting legacy of compassion and understanding.

Surrounding them, the Mystos Realm flourished in the glow of newfound unity. Humans and supernatural creatures lived, worked, and celebrated together, their differences celebrated as sources of strength and richness. Vibrant marketplaces bustled with activity, where mystical artisans displayed their creations alongside human craftsmen. Schools were adorned with art that celebrated the harmonious blend of human and supernatural cultures. Parks echoed with laughter and shared experiences, where families of all kinds found solace and belonging.

The legacy of Lilly and Gabriel's love reverberated throughout the realm, inspiring a new generation to embrace the path of acceptance and compassion. Their story became woven into the fabric of the Mystos Realm, passed down through generations, reminding all who heard it of the enduring power of love to transform lives and shape destinies.

In the twilight of their lives, as they watched the moon rise over the mystical landscape, Lilly and Gabriel found solace in the knowledge that their love had created a lasting bond between the human world and the Mystos Realm. They cherished the memories of their journey, the challenges they had overcome, and the connections they had forged.

Surrounded by loved ones and a community that thrived in harmony, Lilly and Gabriel knew that their legacy would endure beyond their mortal years. Their love, etched in the very fabric of the Mystos Realm, would forever guide its inhabitants towards a future where acceptance, empathy, and unity prevailed.

And as the moonlight bathed them in its ethereal glow, Lilly and Gabriel whispered their gratitude to the universe, embracing the certainty that their love would be remembered, their story immortalized in the hearts of those who believed in the transformative power of love.

In the Mystos Realm, under the moonlit sky, their love would shine forever, a beacon of hope and a testament to the enduring bonds that can be forged when hearts are open and souls unite.